SAND CAKE

❋ A ❋

FRANK ASCH

Bear Story

Parents' Magazine Press ❋ New York

A Parents Magazine
Read Aloud Original

Copyright © 1978 by Frank Asch
All rights reserved
Printed in the United States of America
10 9 8 7 6 5

Library of Congress Cataloging in Publication Data

Asch, Frank.
  Sand cake.

  SUMMARY: Papa Bear uses his culinary
skills and a little imagination to concoct
a sand cake.
  [1. Cake—Fiction. 2. Bears—Fiction]
I. Title.
PZ7.A778San   [E]   78-11183
ISBN 0-8193-0985-0
ISBN 0-8193-0986-9 lib. bdg.

For my dad

One summer day,
the bear family went to the beach
where they swam...

and sunned themselves
on a blanket.

After a while, Baby Bear said
he felt like doing something else.
"If I make you a cake, will you
eat it?" he asked Papa Bear.

"Sure," said Papa Bear.
"If you use flour, milk
and eggs, I will be happy
to eat your cake."

Baby Bear looked around.
All he could see was sand
and water for miles.

"How can I find flour,
and eggs and milk at the
beach?" asked Baby Bear.

"That's easy," said Papa Bear.
"Eggs come from a chicken,

milk comes from a cow,
and flour comes from wheat."

"Well, if it is so easy," said
Baby Bear, "then *you* make a cake
with flour, milk and eggs and
I will eat it."
"Okay," said Papa Bear,
"I will," and he got up and went
down to the water's edge.
He picked up a stick that had
washed up on the beach.

With the stick he drew
a chicken in the wet sand.
Under the chicken he drew an egg.

He scooped up the egg,

and put it in Baby Bear's bucket.

Then he drew some wheat
and ground it up in his hands
to make the flour.
He added the flour to the eggs.

Next, he drew a cow and
under the cow a pail of milk.
He poured the milk into the
bucket with the eggs and flour.

On all of this he sprinkled
some salt from the sea.

Then Papa Bear drew an oven.
Where the oven door was,
he dug a hole and buried
the bucket.

"Come on," he said to
Baby Bear, "let's go for a swim.
By the time we come back, the cake
will be ready for you to eat."

All the time Baby Bear was
swimming, he kept wondering,
"How will I ever be able to
eat that cake?"

When they came out of the water,
Papa Bear dug up the bucket…

and turned it upside down
on the beach.
The cake was done.

"Well now," said Papa Bear,
"are you going to eat the
nice cake I made for you?"

"Sure," said Baby Bear.
He picked up a stick and
drew a picture of himself
around the cake.

"Here I am, and I have eaten
the cake. See it in my stomach?"

Papa Bear laughed and gave
Baby Bear a great big hug.
"Now I am hungry, too,"
he said.

"Then you can both have
some of *my* cake,"
said Mama Bear, and she opened
the picnic basket. "I made mine
with *real* flour, milk and eggs."
And it was delicious!

About the author/artist

Award-winning author/artist of several fanciful picture books, including *Monkey Face,* his first book for Parents', Frank Asch has gained a reputation for his wry and witty tales for young children. He has also taught in a Montessori school and created his own children's theater productions "as a means of communicating directly with young kids."